£6.95

D1344004

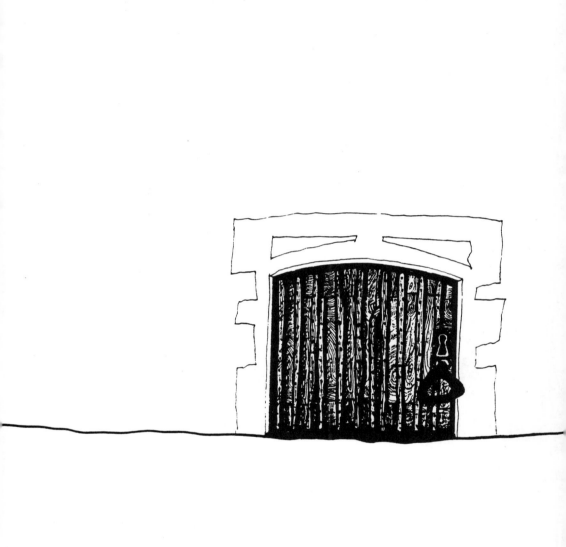

He had been passing the
time practising his signature
on the steamed-up mirror.
Now his bath was getting
cold. Why these tourists
wanted to see his house was
a mystery to him. But why
they wanted to see his
bathroom was absolutely
pig-flighted!

King Kid

with love Rozelle Bentheim xx

Rozelle Bentheim

ABC
London

DEDICATED with love to Steven Gordon & Amadea Bentheim.

Thank you

(in chronological order) Sharon Ellis, Lela White,
Rebecca Mirkin, Gertrude Bentheim (for WPC),
Jancis Robinson, Phillip Thompson, Susan Benn, Rod Hall,
Helen Wire, Lisa Eveleigh, Sue Tarsky, Jennifer Campbell

hello

Katy & Jonathan Steen, Nicky & Lulu Kirk, Julia Middleton
James or Meredith Williams, Laura Molloy, Albertine Rae
Susan Marion Jeen, Tom Browne-Wilkinson, the Lennon children
Larry & Nancy, Emily Hudson, Nicky Esdaille, Isabel Gibson
Nicholas Gnushkin, Oliver & Miles Hillier, Joe Foster
Rachel & Nicky Smith, Hannah Thornton-Smith, Felix Descamps
Sam & Lottie, Minnie, Lola, Mary & Anna, Teddy O'Conner
Jaspreet, Gurpreet & Satnam Panesar, all the Caplan children

Text and illustrations copyright © 1991 Rozelle Bentheim
The moral right of the author has been asserted.

First published in 1991 by **A**B**C**, **A**ll **B**ooks for **C**hildren,
a division of The All Children's Company Ltd
33 Museum Street, London WC1A 1LD

Printed and bound in Hong Kong

British Library Cataloguing in Publication Data
Bentheim, Rozelle
King Kid
I. Title
823.914 [J]

ISBN 1-85406-113-5

my Monster

my monster is called slimey.
He smashes everything in sight.
He has got two eyes in his tummy
They are as big as two
classrooms.
He has got one hand and he
has spikes EVERYWHERE.
He has got teeth in
his hand.

by

FOR SALE

Joseph Lenthal

WANTED

Jamie Rust

WANT TO WRITE?

Joseph Lenthal

normal Brides maids

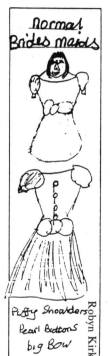

Puffy Shoalders
Pearl Bottons
big Bow

Robyn Kirk

EXPERIENCED ☆ WIZARD ☆

seeks interesting work.
I am tired of doing boring spells and
want a challenge. (I am very cheap.)

SALE

Jessica Lenthal

LOST

Alexander Pearce

FOUND

Nicholas Pearce

LOST

Chloe Parsons

Chapter 1

Sitting in bed, King Kid stared at the cold Brussels sprout he had to finish from supper and willed it to vanish. He re-read the Wizard's advert. As he picked up the sprout and forced himself to chew it, he wondered if this advert could change his life.

King Kid remembered how sad he and Spike the Cactus had been when the King Dad had been eaten — as sad as a boy and his pet cactus could be. Spike the Cactus had eventually managed to cheer him up a micro bit by pointing out that he was now KING Kid — no longer only a normal kid. Therefore, he was entitled to King-type privileges, such as eating chips and chocolate for breakfast, having unlimited pocket money, and imprisoning a big sister.

But, there was no difference so far. He still had to eat porridge for breakfast, have only two pence pocket money, and his big sister was still on the loose, being uncontrollably sensible. Then Spike the Cactus suggested that although he had failed to 'King' grown-ups, he must be able to King-command children. King Kid was outraged, but he thought he would try it — only to see if it would work.

Just before lessons on Monday morning, he stood on a desk in front of the whole class, feeling very nervous, as bad as those waiting-to-show-the-teacher-homework-that-you-haven't-done feelings. Taking a deep breath, he commanded in a booming voice like kings do in films: "Hello and shut up! Now, I am King Kid, I command: 1. that you always let ME choose teams; 2. that you always let ME go to the head of the crisps queue; and, 3. that you always let ME sit at the front of the school bus!"

They laughed at him. King Kid had an uneasy

feeling that Spike the Cactus was a bit too ambitious.

When King Kid wasn't allowed to have a dog (It would smell the antiques) or a cat (would scratch the tourists) or a goldfish (too wild), he had thought that the pet cactus his mother had given him for his birthday was an insult. But quite the reverse. Spike was easy to carry, house-trained, didn't require a lot of water and had surprisingly enterprising ideas—for a houseplant.

As King Kid managed to swallow the last particles of sprout, his eyes refocussed on the television screen. On the stage of a packed auditorium, Jay Cloth, the heavy metal pop star, stamped his feet to the beat of his roaring music. The fans were completely under his spell. The left side of the audience leaped up with his left foot. The right side of the audience leaped up with his right foot. King Kid was impressed.

"I bet Jay Cloth and the Knuckle Dusters don't have any problems getting people to do what they want. People probably beg for the chance to help them out. I have to wait for grown-ups to stop blabbing before I can ask for anything and then they only listen if I say please a hundred times. And then they say No anyway."

King Kid tore out the wizard's advert. He put Spike in its oven-glove, and put on his dressing gown. He was going to see that wizard right this minute!

Chapter 2

On the Wizard's doorstep.

DING DONG!

Rita Lovely, the Wizard's enthusiastic
trainee, answered the door.

"Good evening and shut up! I am King Kid!"

"Is that a crown or is your head a funny shape?"
replied Rita.

"I command you to let me in. Spike the Cactus has
come about the Wizard's advert," King Kid insisted.

"Oh, well, Spike the Cactus had better come in
then," Rita Lovely said as she took Spike and slammed
the door.

DING DONG!

King Kid rang the bell again.

"What is it now?"

"Spike the Cactus does not have legs and cannot
speak."

"Really?"

"I do the walking and talking for Spike. He commands you to let me in, too," King Kid said hopefully.

Rita slammed the door.

D I N G   D O N G !

"I want to come in!"

"Not until you say the password. It's a word starting with PL and ending with EASE."

King Kid thought hard. "Plum Fleas?"

"I want to come in PLEASE!" Rita was losing her patience.

"But YOU are in," King Kid replied, exasperated.

Rita tried again. "You want to come in — PLEASE!"

"Yes, that's what I said when I got here," King Kid said and walked past her.

Rita sighed and led King Kid into the Wizard's Consulting Room.

The Wizard bowed till his nose brushed the carpet.

"Your Mini Majesty, your Royal Shortness, what can I, your crawliest subject, do for you?"

King Kid thought what a nice person the Wizard was.

"I have come to order a spell. I do not want a spell for

myself, of course. It is my pet, Spike the Cactus, that wants it. If you help Spike, I shall help you, seeing Spike is my pet." King Kid winked at the Wizard.

"What Spike wants is a spell that will make ME a proper, bossy king. Spike the Cactus wants:

1. that my friends will play the games that
   I want and let ME win;
2. that grown-ups will do what I want
   for a change; and,
3. that my mother will not make ME
   sing with the Goody Goody Two
   Shoes at the Palace Christmas Concert;
   or make ME give soppy flowers TO and
   be kissed BY Dame Bertha Innuendo,
   the hugely famous opera singer.

"By the way, Spike wants me to sing with Jay Cloth and the Knuckle Dusters. That is what Spike the Cactus wants. Spike says, get spelling because Spike needs this fixed soon, so make it quick."

"Nothing could be easier, my Crown-ed Kiddy. I shall telephone you to make a further appointment. Goodbye."

Chapter 3

The Wizard could hardly believe his luck. "King Kid wants me to make a spell for him, or is he only King-Kidding?

"A Royal spell could transform my life. Chemists and computers leave very little for us wizards to do these days. People only want goose-pimply-nasty, jaw-droppingly-spiteful curses written. I don't know if they work, but they certainly cheer my customers up.

"King Kid is sure to make me Royal Wizard . . . I can

see it now. A Royal Gala Film Premiere . . . of a film made in celebration of ME!" The Wizard smiled. "I arrive in my solid gold helicopter. A flunkey rushes to open the door nearly getting his head sheared off by its spinning blades. Only one of my shining shoes has to appear on the red carpet for the mass of adoring fans to burst into applause. Camera flashes blind me as I descend, waving at the wall of enraptured faces, packed, row upon row, like a stack of pink and brown ping-pong balls."

The Wizard sat down and put his feet up. "Now, I am aboard my yacht, digesting a light banquet, amusing myself by accepting compliments lavished upon me by admirers. And the gifts they have brought me! Each trying to outdo the other to win my attention — mink sofas, ostrich-feather pyjamas and golden lavatory seats!"

"Where is The Spell Book, Wizard?" Rita asked.

"Rita, you had better call me Sir Wizard . . ."

"Is it in the filing cabinet?"

". . . or perhaps Grand Wizard?"

"You had better make sure that you find the right spell and don't change that kid into a dustbin or you'll get called a . . . . wizard!"

"Gulp!"

Chapter 4

King Kid was thinking, "If only my mother, the Queen, Mrs Queenie Royal, had not opened the palace to tourists, 'partly to raise money and partly to prevent pride'. I hate it — picnickers all over the palace; frilly little girls in my room playing with my Mashing Monster and Space Bashers; and all those ladies smiling at me, asking me daft grown-ups-trying-to-get-children-to-like-them questions and then trying to KISS me. And this year's Christmas Concert — to have to sing with the Goody Goody Two Shoes is bad enough, but to be kissed by that big wobbly woman of the opera, Dame Bertha Innuendo! Ugh! The spell must put an end to my nightmare.

"In the war against grown-ups, kids always lose. But kings always win wars, that's how they get to be kings in the first place — by being bossier than anyone else. I'm a King Kid and I still lose. It's not fair. Please make it that I am spelled into a proper, bossy king! If I were a proper king I could sing with Jay Cloth and the Knuckle

Dusters at the Palace Concert, on a huge stage with spotlights and giant microphones. We'd roar onto the stage on massive motorbikes, dressed in black leather with chains and gauntlets . . . And I wouldn't have to kiss ANYONE."

"Lunch is ready. Come to the table."

"I'm busy."

"Now!"

"In a minute!"

"Not in a minute, now!"

"See what I mean, Spike?"

Ch^ap^te^r 5

Rita Lovely was cross. She had expected training as a wizard's assistant to be exciting. But the Wizard always had her doing what he called Women's House Magic — cleaning and shopping. The most magic she had seen in this house was the carrots expanding in her mug of vegetable cuppa-soup.

The Royal Spell would be her first chance to try real magic and she was not going to let the Wizard ruin it.

She opened the index of The Spell Book, found a magnifying glass and set about finding the correct spell amongst the millions of entries.

Two days later, Rita found the right spell and wheeled over the massive book. "Look, Wizard, ELIXIR, a tincture or cordial able to transform one thing into another. Varieties: Gold — from metal into. Jelly — jellied eels into jelly babies. Life — Eternal Life, Half Life, Lifestyle — various improvements (see Sunday supplement). This is what you need, an Elixir of Lifestyle. The recipe is on pages 703,286 and 703,287."

"Look it up, Rita, and order the ingredients from Mail Order Magic immediately."

Chapter 6

The next day a heavy box arrived from Mail Order Magic. The Wizard was having difficulty opening it.

"Rita, find me a screwdriver. Then you can take the day off. I need some peace and quiet to examine and put away this magic shopping."

"Typical! This is the first shopping he has ever put away in his life. He wants to keep the excitement of unwrapping the spell ingredients all to himself." Rita found the toolbox. "If he were a proper wizard, this screwdriver would find him!"

She put on her coat, slammed the front door, and left to visit her dad, the Kingdom Librarian.

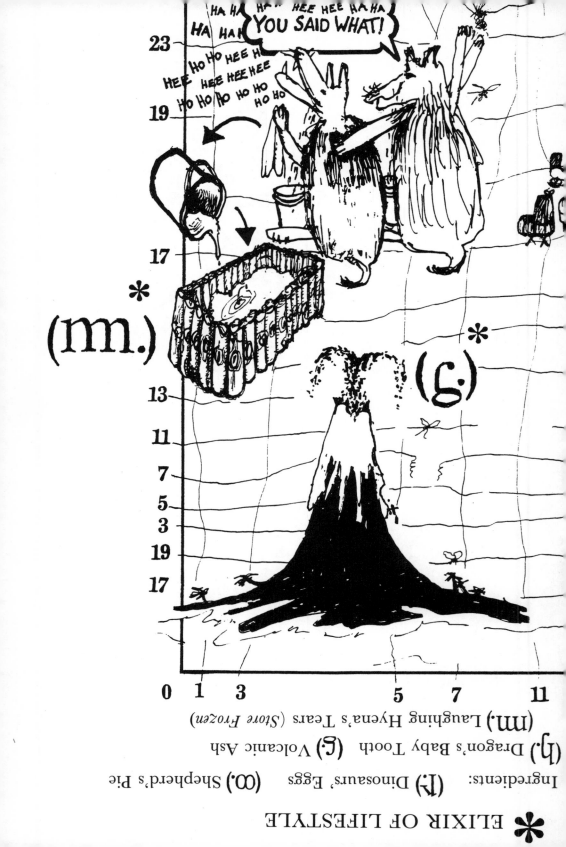

IMPORTANT

Ref.: The Elixir
For the elixir to work
on King Kid, this
recipe will need a strand
of his hair.
It must be taken from him
by surprise.
Any ideas?
See you tomorrow,
Rita.

(♮.)*

(∞.)*

(♭.)*

23

The Wizard read the note and
scratched his head.

"Oh, fishspit!"

Chapter 7

In the Wizard's Consulting Room, the clock struck four.
Outside, it was snowing. Cold crept in under the doors.
The Wizard shivered. After unwrapping all those
ingredients he felt in need of a snooze. But he had
work to do, hard work, hard thought-catching work!
He had to find, trap and catch an idea that would
enable him to steal a strand of King Kid's hair without
getting caught. "Let me see if I can recall my Thought-
catching Procedure. Ah, yes! . . . First—Preparation."
The Wizard got busy. He put on his slippers, made a
large mug of cocoa, went into the Consulting Room,
stoked the fire and brought out his stash of
chocolate—and had a rest. "What's next? . . . Action!"
He stuffed all the chocolate into his mouth and drank

cocoa, whilst chanting, "mmmMMMmmm!" and put on his Thinking-cap. It was metal and pointed, with an aerial to catch any interesting thoughts that might float by. The Wizard was waiting very hard, thinking that he needed a longer aerial, when he started to receive something. Heeeeeeeeee! But not a word, stray thought, idea nor even a daydream followed. The heeeeeeee sound only repeated itself over and over again. "There must be some static jamming my brain waves." He listened harder. A fly flew past. "That's strange, my aerial must be picking up the fly buzzing." He gave the aerial a tap. The sound was getting louder. Haahaahaa! "Oh, this is ridiculous. It's no use. Too much insect interference!" He took the Thinking-cap off. But, to his amazement, he could still hear the noise. He shook his head. He poked his ears. But he could still hear it. Hoo Hoo Hooo, Haa Haa Haaa, Hee Hee Heee! He realised it was something much, much bigger than a fly. "Oh, I know what it is. Rita must have left the radio on, careless girl!" But the radio was not on. Hoo Hoo Hooo, Haa Haa Haaa, Hee Hee Heee! Was something laughing at him? "It's those kids next door spying on me again!" He got up to shoo them away but the street was empty. Hoo Hoo Hooo, Haa Haa Haaa, Hee Hee Heee! The Wizard buried his head in the cushions. Each

Ha Ha crashed into the next Hoo Hoo Hooo and bounced up and down on his eardrums. "Who- or whatever you are making this head-spinning din, go and make it somewhere else!"

The Wizard tried to remain calm! He sat up and listened. He was sure the noise was coming from this room. Beginning at the door, he studied everything, scanning from floor to ceiling. Nothing in the bookcase . . . nothing on the filing cabinets . . . and then he saw it. It was on the mantlepiece, where he had put it. It was shaking with laughter! The bamboo box from Mail Order Magic was rippling like a concertina, splitting its sides with hoo-hoo-ing and ha-ha-ing. The box spat and hissed. Droplets of sticky liquid clung to its lid and when they finally let go, they fell into the fire, exploding in fits of giggles. "Oh, fishspit! It's alive!" he shrieked and ran into the hall. The Wizard slammed the door shut and locked it. He rummaged through the Mail Order Magic packaging. The bamboo box must have had a label. But there was nothing. He sat back, flustered and afraid. The laughter was getting more and more raucous. Rrrrring-Ring! The Wizard jumped into his skin and shut his eyes tight. Rrrrring-Ring! It was only the telephone. His neighbour was complaining about the noise. Then the Wizard saw a crumpled postcard lying on the floor. On one side there was a colour photograph of a very serious-looking Laughing Hyena, and on the reverse a carefully written message:

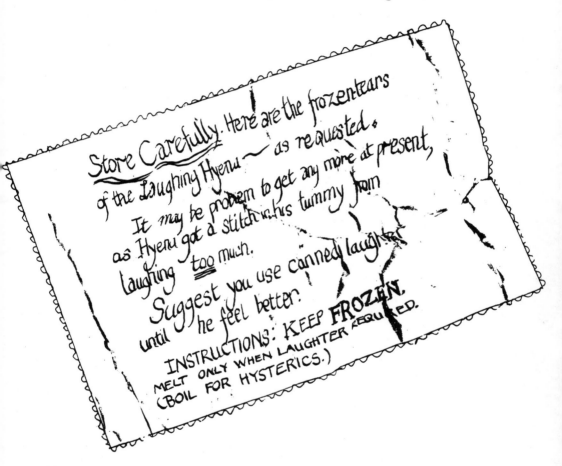

Store Carefully. Here are the frozen tears of the Laughing Hyena ~ as requested. It may be problem to get any more at present, as Hyena got a stitch in his tummy from laughing **too** much. Suggest you use canned laughter until he feel better.

INSTRUCTIONS: KEEP **FROZEN**. MELT ONLY WHEN LAUGHTER REQUIRED. (BOIL FOR HYSTERICS.)

The Wizard unlocked the door and ran into the Consulting Room, picked up a wastepaper bin, knocked the writhing box into it and put the lot in the fridge to cool down.

Chapter 8

Rita Lovely and her dad
were sharing a chocolate
biscuit at his desk in the
Kingdom Library when they
heard hooting and tooting
and the screeching of brakes.
Rita stuck her head
out of the window.

On the motorway below,
several drivers had pulled onto the
hard shoulder and were using
rude words and shaking their
fists at a many-yeared man
dressed in a yellow woolly
jumpsuit and mini-cape.
The many-yeared man was
making his way gracefully
through the zooming lanes-and-lanes-
and-lanes of traffic—somersaulting, pirouetting
and crook-vaulting over speeding vehicles;
flashing his mini-cape at fearsome lorry

drivers; avoiding, in unusual and creative ways, being knocked over. He smiled defiantly at the oncoming drivers, leaped over their cars, and bowed

triumphantly to the backs of their astonished heads. A dog and a sheep followed him, copying his every move. The vintage man often had to interrupt some particularly colourful sequence of car-leaping, to scoop up his less-skilled, four-legged companions from beneath the rampant wheels of a ten ton truck.

"Dad, who is that man?"

"Oh, that will be my old friend, Gra-a-assy Scubs, the shepherd, moving his flock to their autumn roundabout. He comes this way when it gets chillier, so he has less of a bus ride home." Gra-a-assy Scubs was the last shepherd in the Kingdom. His pastures were any bits of green he could find: roundabouts, motorway verges, midnight raids into back gardens — anything to keep his sheep healthy and happy. Shepherding was tough, difficult and dangerous. A fact that the three brave companions knew to their cost. For Shepherd Scubs now had only one sheep — a fine, bold seasoned, mischievous sheep with a limp, one eye and a hearty appetite.

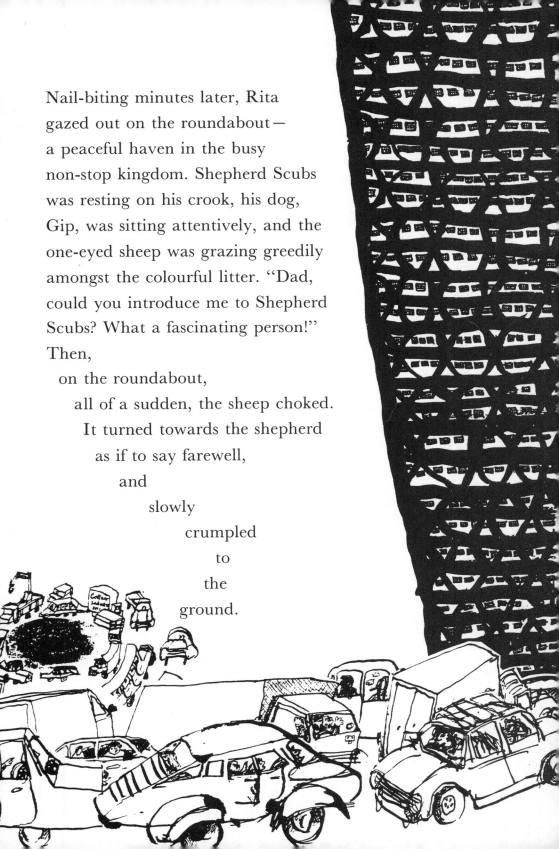

Nail-biting minutes later, Rita
gazed out on the roundabout—
a peaceful haven in the busy
non-stop kingdom. Shepherd Scubs
was resting on his crook, his dog,
Gip, was sitting attentively, and the
one-eyed sheep was grazing greedily
amongst the colourful litter. "Dad,
could you introduce me to Shepherd
Scubs? What a fascinating person!"
Then,
  on the roundabout,
    all of a sudden, the sheep choked.
     It turned towards the shepherd
      as if to say farewell,
       and
        slowly
         crumpled
         to
         the
         ground.

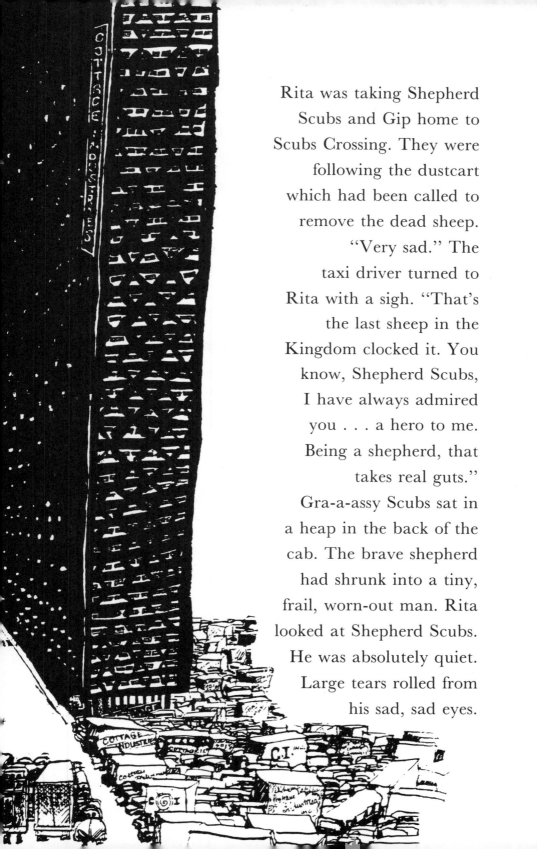

Rita was taking Shepherd
Scubs and Gip home to
Scubs Crossing. They were
following the dustcart
which had been called to
remove the dead sheep.
"Very sad." The
taxi driver turned to
Rita with a sigh. "That's
the last sheep in the
Kingdom clocked it. You
know, Shepherd Scubs,
I have always admired
you . . . a hero to me.
Being a shepherd, that
takes real guts."
Gra-a-assy Scubs sat in
a heap in the back of the
cab. The brave shepherd
had shrunk into a tiny,
frail, worn-out man. Rita
looked at Shepherd Scubs.
He was absolutely quiet.
Large tears rolled from
his sad, sad eyes.

Chapter 9

King Kid had been practising bowing in the bathroom for twenty minutes.

". . . Spike, when I am a proper and bossy king, Jay Cloth will be my best friend. Ahem. Jay, awesome concert, man, really awesome! And jamming with you? It's not rubbish!"

King Kid pulled the chain, ssspppplllaaasssshhh, and bowed.

"Oh please, fans, no more."

King Kid pulled the chain, ssspppplllaaasssshhh, and bowed.

"Hush, fans!"

And again, ssspppplllaaasssshhh.

Ssspppplllaaasssshhh! "Thank you fans."

Sssspppplllllaaaasssssshhhh! "Thank you."

Ssssssppppppplllllllaaaaaasssssshhhhh! "No, really, fans! Too awesome!"

Chapter 10

In the bowling alley, King Kid's big sister, Princess Princess, was crossing the polished wooden floor, using old newspapers as stepping stones. Before sitting down next to her friend, she covered the seat with a newspaper because she was so dirty. Princess Princess was always filthy because she was a Social Climber.

Princess Princess had wanted to be a mountaineer but all the mountains in the Kingdom had been flattened to make car parks. So she climbed the monster cottage scrapers. Their thatched roofs were the closest thing to real countryside left in the Kingdom. There was some wildlife up there: a little moss, several weeds and a protected pair of sparrows.

The monster cottage scrapers were coated with a grimy, sticky deposit from the exhaust fumes of thousands of cars. Although exhilarating, climbing them was difficult, slippery and soiling (the Princess had to paint her fingernails black). It was probably just like scaling the insides of a smoker's lungs.

But there were compensations. Social Climbing gave Princess the chance to meet people. Office workers were usually quite friendly once they got over the shock of seeing her dangling outside their windows. They would call out to each other, "No need to worry, if it's someone that dirty it must be the Princess." If they weren't busy, they would ask her in for a wash and a cup of tea.

CHAPTER 11

The Smallest Hair Casts Its Shadow

GOETHE

FILOSPELL DAY PLANNER

Friday 13

___ Make URGENT list.

___ How much do golden helicopters cost?

___ Send my life story to the Kingdom Film Company.

___ List what presents I want for Christmas and send copies to friends, relatives and Rita.

___ Attain one hair from King Kid's head without his knowledge.

___ Remember to tell Rita about the Frozen Hyena's Tears in the ice box.

___ Put up central heating.

Friday 13   RITA'S ACTION LIST
Tick off as task completed.

Objectives:
✓ 1. Think of a new career.
✓ 2. File newt's eggs.
✓ 3. Solve problem: Work out how to
      remove a hair from King Kid's
      head without him knowing.
SOLUTION: Arrange Pre-Spell check-up
at a time when he is very sleepy.

DO:
✓ Persuade Wizard to follow my plan.
✓ Telephone King Kid to make a secret
  midnight appointment at Palace.
✓ Wash my costume.
✓ Wash magic carpet.
✓ Wash Wizard.
✓ Curl mice's fur.
✓ Check all magic equipment in good
  working order.
✓ Order taxi to take us to palace and
  bring us home again.
DEFROST FRIDGE :
✓ Switch off.
✓ Leave all fridge doors open.
✓ Especially ice box.
✓ Leave bowl of boiling water in fridge
  (to speed up defrosting).

Chapter 12

The Palace scraper was the tallest building in the Kingdom. Rita was thrilled to be standing up there, alone, on its roof. She was so high up that the air smelt almost cleanish and she was sure that she could see passengers waving to her from the aeroplane that thundered past.

Beneath her, the city looked very different. She looked down onto the roofs of the cottage scrapers. They looked like the little fields she had seen in story-books. Once upon a time the earth must have been very, very beautiful.

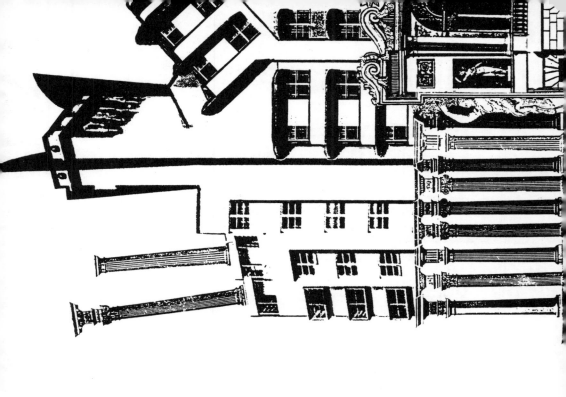

Rita looked at her watch. It was quarter to midnight. She had finished taking out the mice's curlers. They were now in their cage waiting for supper, trying to outdo each other over who was the hungriest and who had the longest tongue. Rita unpacked the rest of the equipment ready for King Kid's Pre-Spell Check-up. She hoped he would be half asleep during it so that it would be far less risky for them to steal a strand of his hair.

Rita had just lit the fire-breathing dragon heater and put on soft, spooky music, when King Kid arrived. His bed had been very warm and cosy and he was very sleepy, but he needed the spell and he needed it badly. The day of the Palace Concert was drawing nearer and he didn't want to have to put Plan B into action and risk not getting any Christmas presents.

Place the edge of this drawing against a mirror to see the complete picture of the Palace scraper.

He hardly recognised the roof. "Oh Spike, I wish I'd brought my camera. Prick me and tell me I'm not dreaming." He was just about to ask Rita, when she put a finger to her lips and gently sat him in the Wizarding Chair. This was made out of a stuffed, knitted tiger but articulated like a dentist's chair.

Pulling a rolled carpet towards King Kid, she began to recite softly. "In the days of Kublai Khan, there were many, marvellous, magical mysteries; there were flying carpets . . ." Rita gave the carpet an extra tug and the Wizard rolled out and jumped up. He fixed King Kid with a hypnotic stare and whispered, "But that was in the old days. Now, we have jets and fitted carpets and magic has to fit each task SAFELY, no tripping up! No flying off the broom handle! Oh Tiny Highness, I shall have to test your resistance to magic.

I shall do that using a very SECRET and EXPENSIVE instrument, the *Magibeama Counter*, so secret that we shall have to blindfold both you and Spike." They were not taking any risks. "Rita, put on the blindfolds! You may experience strange sensations, but I ask you not to question them. Magic rays can feel very tingly, so please, Micro Master, respond normally."

King Kid nodded. He was having difficulty staying awake. The tiger chair was so soft . . . .

When King Kid was safely blindfolded, the Wizard and Rita got to work—silently.

Rita took off King Kid's slippers, opened a tub of cheese spread and smeared cheese all over the soles of King Kid's feet.

The Wizard unpacked a large pair of fisherman's socks and his fishing tackle.

Place the edge of this drawing against a mirror to see the complete picture of the Palace scraper.

He attached a small clip
to the end of his fishing
line. Rita fetched the
fisherman's socks
and put King Kid's
cheesed feet inside
them. She gave
the Wizard
a thumbs-up.

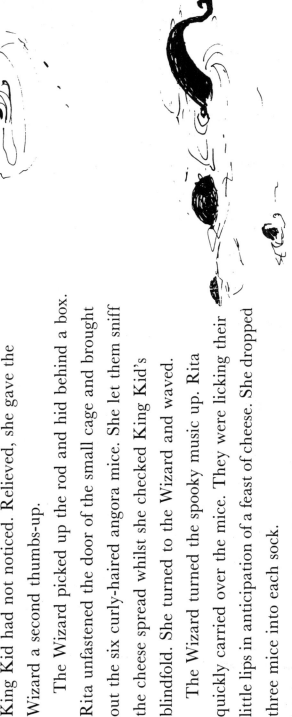

Rita unwound the fishing line, cautiously selected one strand of King Kid's hair and caught it in the clip. King Kid had not noticed. Relieved, she gave the Wizard a second thumbs-up.

The Wizard picked up the rod and hid behind a box. Rita unfastened the door of the small cage and brought out the six curly-haired angora mice. She let them sniff the cheese spread whilst she checked King Kid's blindfold. She turned to the Wizard and waved.

The Wizard turned the spooky music up. Rita quickly carried over the mice. They were licking their little lips in anticipation of a feast of cheese. She dropped three mice into each sock.

As soon as they landed, the mice began to lick the cheesed soles of King Kid's feet as fast as their long tongues would allow. King Kid jumped up in the air. The strand of his hair, fixed to the fishing line, was pulled free. The Wizard wound in the line and landed King Kid's stolen hair.

Place the edge of this drawing against a mirror to see the complete picture of the Palace scraper.

Chapter 13

Time: 01.00 KINGDOM HOUR

IN SPACE
Planets are born and die. A lonely firework travels its aimless pa

The earth spins on its axis.

IN THE KINGDOM
King Kid is back in bed, fast asleep, after successfully passing th

a nightmare—he is wearing his flopsy bunny sleepsuit. He has a large

Dame Bertha Innuendo flings open the classroom door, rushes in

massive mirror and a gigantic lipstick! She is putting on coats an

The Wizard and Rita are in a taxi on their way home

was an excellent ruse and now I have the hair I can go ahead

future Royal Wizard. Isn't that exciting?" "Oh, very!" Rita

stopped by a police roadblock. "Good evening lady and

further." "Why? My house is only around the corner," replied the

there is a beast on the loose. We have taken the precaution of

to worry. We believe that we have tracked the beast down to ar

For a little beast it certainly makes an infernal racket. Listen,

HhhhhhhhHHHHEEEEeeeeeHHHHHHhhhhheeee

At Scubs Crossing, his little house on the traffic island

"My first, my number 1 . . . that would be Able . . . bought

little runt he was . . . grew into a fine big ram . . . da-aaa-addi

engine . . . unfortunate, but I suppose old Able gave his life that

IN GLASGOW
A sad man stands on a hill, watching the night sky for a comet.

o infinity past drifting space rubbish. A spacecraft is on course.

izard's test, but he is tossing and turning. King Kid is having
bunch of pink roses in his hands. He is standing in front of his class!
and grabs the flowers! She opens her huge handbag and takes out a
oats of red lipstick. She is preparing to . . . KISS HIM!

from the Palace. The Wizard is very pleased. "That pre-spell check
with The Elixir. If you are good, Rita, you may assist the Kingdom's
replied. They were nearing the Wizard's street, when they were
gentleman," said the policeman, "I am afraid that you can go no
Vizard. "It is for your own personal safety, sir. We believe that
evacuating the area and calling out the army. There is no need
ice box not very far from here and we have the fridge surrounded.

there it goes again."

HHhhhaaaahhhhaaaaa! The Wizard fainted.

Shepherd Scubs is trying to sleep, counting sheep.
from old farmer Oats when he was a little la-aaa-aaa-mby . . . scrawny
many little ones, he did . . . Let me see . . . he was hit by a fire
others might live . . . it's an ill wind . . . zzzzz."

Time: 03.00 KINGDOM HOURS

IN SPACE
Planets die and are born. The lonely firework travels on past the spac[e]
drinking a can of Coca-Cola. The earth turns on its axis.

IN THE KINGDOM
In **King Kid's** nightmare, Dame Bertha Innuendo is bearing
a laughing stock for the rest of his life! When, all of a sudden, the
a straw in it. "Drink this quickly, Mega Majesty." As King Kid
In the police cell, the Wizard's face is ashen. A solitary electric
Hideous shadows are cast by the bodies of last summer's
not bothering to disguise the fact that she thinks he is a total idio[t]
hooves muddy . . . would only eat daisies . . . what was her full title . . .
Lamb . . . right little madam, ran off with that American, Rambo."

IN GLASGOW
The sad man still watches the night sky for a comet.

returns to the spacecraft. He leaves the empty can in space. He is the

y Cloth roars in on his motor bike. The class is astonished when Jay
with him at the Palace Christmas Concert. Detective Sergeant Lily
Wizard, in short, you left home this evening rolled up in a carpet,
re 'unaware that Ms Lovely was defrosting the fridge'. Ms Lovely
as you, sir, had failed to enlighten her. Consequently, the Laughing
tter of hours your neighbours ran in terror from their homes
thieves free to don their ear plugs and get busy! They must have
is episode because of the involvement of a Royal Person. But,
"zzz . . . 123rd . . . that would be Mutton Rothschild . . . was interested
brain . . . pity about that army lorry . . . zzz . . ."

dawn is approaching.

rubbish. The spacecraft stops, its hatch opens, an astronaut floats out,

down on him! The whole class is giggling. This is the end! He will be
Wizard jumps out of a desk and gives King Kid a test-tube with
rinks The Elixir he calls out defiantly, "Go hug a slug, big kisser!"
bulb generates a hard, white light through a greasy plastic shade.
toasted moths. Detective Sergeant Lily Tightgrip is staring at him,
"... my 63rd sheep ... fine lady she was ... didn't like getting her
came from good stock though ... Lady Something ... Lady Caroline

IN SPACE

Planets are born and die. The lonely firework travels on. The astronaut
first space litter bug in the galaxy. The earth turns on its axis.

IN THE KINGDOM

King Kid is now dreaming that the classroom door bursts open a
Cloth dismounts, falls to his knees, and begs King Kid to perform
Tightgrip put down her notebook. "To conclude your statement,
having turned up the central heating." She gave him a look. "Yo
tells us that she did not know that it contained Frozen Hyena's Tears,
Hyena's Tears began to melt, emitting spine-chilling laughter. In a
to my station to seek the protection of my officers—leaving the local
thought Christmas had come early. This time, I shall have to overloo
Mr Wizard ... I shall be watching ... and waiting."
in nature ... particularly fleas ... was a pacifist ... zzz ... fir

IN GLASGOW

The sad man still stands on the hill and waits for the comet but

Time: 07.00 KINGDOM HOURS

IN SPACE

Planets die and are born. The lonely firework passes out of th
Stanley. The Coca-Cola can orbits the earth whilst the earth

IN THE KINGDOM

King Kid woke up. "Morning Spike . . . What? . . . You sugges
a cool costume for playing with Jay and the boys at the Palace
the ice box to check that the Hyena's Tears were frozen solid
me. Your carelessness could have spoilt my chance of making
my opportunity to become one of the most revered, fawned-upo
You're fired!" Rita let the pot of tea she was making smash to
rucksack and left. "589th . . . zzz . . . that would have bee
zzz zzzzzzzzz . . ."

IN GLASGOW

The sad man stands on the hill, disappointed, and watches the sun rise.
his faith in surprises. In space the sun is eclipsed by

alaxy. The spacecraft begins its long journey home to the planet

ırns on its axis.

at I had better go to The Royal Tailors immediately to order

gig? Good idea!" **The Wizard** strode into the kitchen. He opened

"Well, Rita, see where your obsession with kitchen hygiene has got

The Elixir for the King. Your blind stupidity nearly ruined

autograph-most-in-demand Grand Wizards in the universe.

the floor. "Go cuddle an octopus!" she roared, picked up her

e Queen of Sheepa . . . zzz . . . cement mixer . . . zzz . . . zzz

Vhen, to his astonishment, he sees the sun eclipsed. This restores

e Coca-Cola can.

Chapter 14

Shepherd Gabriel Scubs had not had a good night. He was missing his sheep.

From his bedroom over the traffic island, he could hear the beginnings of the Kingdom rush hour. He lay there, dreading going downstairs to the toilet and having to cross the river of commuters that poured through his little house at Scubs Crossing.

Living on a major pedestrian crossing had its disadvantages. Shepherd Scubs had to leave his front and back door open for the public. They followed the black-and-white-striped carpet through his hall, rushing in and out of his house. Some people were very kind and dropped in milk and papers; most didn't even notice that they were walking through someone's home. The rush hour was the worst. One morning, Shepherd Scubs couldn't get out of the toilet for an hour.

Shepherd Scubs grimaced. He must go downstairs before the crowds started. He put on his slippers and patted his dog. "Come on Gip, let's brave it."

Meanwhile, King Kid was on his way to The Royal Tailors, in disguise. He didn't want his mother to know where he was going — it might make her suspicious.

Crossing the frozen Palace Pond, he slipped, crashed into the bank and landed on a frog, squashing its leg. He took the frog to the All Heart Hospital Casualty Department. And now he was running late.

It's tricky wearing sunglasses on a dull rainy morning, especially when you're in a hurry. He walked on a dog mess, knocked over a toddler, told a lamppost off for not looking where it was going, and, now, he had gone upstairs instead of *through* Scubs Crossing.

"Oh, Spike. See what you've made me do." He took off his sunglasses and found himself in a small room with a dishevelled bed in the corner. The room had a sad feel to it. "I didn't know anybody lived here." He quickly put on his glasses, pulled down his balaclava, and ran downstairs.

Neville Plush, manager of The Royal Tailors (established 1066) had been watching a small figure for several minutes. He saw sticky fingers trying to find the door, making a greasy trail along his sparkling plate glass window (£1500, window cleaning £1000 per annum).

Neville examined the short person's shoes (local chemist's summer sale £3.50), khaki socks (salvage shop 40p), ladies leather gloves (jumble sale—June, two years ago—the-everything-under-£1 bin), dark glasses (Tony's Bargain Basement 50p), balaclava (army surplus £1.50), trenchcoat (Willet's Sale—three years ago—£15 reduced to £8.50). He especially noticed a large bulge in the right hand pocket . . . a gun-shaped bulge?

The short person opened the door. "Hello and shut up!"

Neville put up his hands.

King Kid was puzzled by the man's behaviour but thought it polite to ignore it. "I am King Kid," he announced, taking off his disguise. "I am appearing in the Palace Christmas Concert, you know. Show me something slick. "

Neville's face glowed with relief.

"Certainly, Sir! I had the pleasure
of outfitting your father."

URGENT

TO WIZARD

expect fixing soonest
M. insists on reher_
sels sicuashon

KRITIKILL

PS better taste
nice

 # Chapter 15

"I'm supposed to be making a spell, not a sweetie," mumbled the Wizard as he read the letter. He tied up his dirty breakfast things in a tablecloth. This was his way of vanishing mess since Rita had walked out. He looked at the other bundles of dishes and wondered whether he should put them in the sink or in the washing-machine.

"Of course, when I am Spellmaker-the-Fabulous, I shan't have to waste my time on such crumby problems!"

He opened The Spell Book and began to assemble all the ingredients: Volcanic Ash, Dragon's Baby Teeth, Dinosaurs' Eggs, Frozen Hyena's Tears (he'd defrost them at the last minute), the shepherd's pie and the King's hair. He took a deep breath, "Now I'm ready to begin."

ELIXIR OF LIFESTYLE **Serves one subject.**

1. Put two teaspoons of Volcanic Ash into a non-stick cauldron.

2. Add 35mm of the subject's hair.

3. Add one chunk of Frozen Hyena's Tears and cover immediately.

4. Heat slowly over a gentle flame to keep the noise down.

5. Add three ground Dragon's Baby Teeth to the flaky crust in the bottom of the cauldron.

6. Put on a pair of rubber gloves and prise open the barrel of Dinosaurs' Eggs.

7. Slide your hands into the barrel. It will feel like bad trifle.

8. It is bad trifle. Feel around for what you hope is an egg (it will be soft and slippery). Trap one against the side of the barrel.

> The Wizard felt something wet ooze
> down the inside of his glove . . .

9. Cup your hands and drag the egg out. Drop it into a bucket where it will bounce to a standstill.

10. Smelly, isn't it? Quickly close the barrel and hold your nose.

11. Run into the garden.

12. Under no circumstances return to the house until fumes have subsided. This may take some time!

13. To open the dinosaur egg,

The Wizard had hoped that he would only

have to hard-boil the egg and use it as a garnish.

. . . pierce the tough slimy shell with a skewer.

14. Squeeze the egg to extract grey, glutinous stuff and little green yolks. This should look like mouldy rice pudding with rotten canned peas in it. If it doesn't, the egg is bad and you must discard it.

"I hope I don't have to separate the yolks
from the grey and beat them till stiff."
He did! (15)

16. Fold in the grey, glutinous stuff.

17. Leave the foul elixir vigorously curdling in the pot. Make yourself a cup of tea and re-read the recipe to check that you have not missed anything.

18. IMPORTANT - For Royalty only, add a freshly minced frog's leg.

"A frog's leg! Mail Order Magic
didn't send a frog's leg."

—————— **TASTY TIPS** ——————

This elixir tastes, well, to be quite honest, we don't know how it tastes - we never dared to make it. If you want someone to actually drink this stuff, the only possible way to make it taste nice is to add a shepherd's eye.

"A shepherd's eye!" The Wizard glared at the Shepherd's pie and hurled it into the dustbin.

Chapter 16

The Wizard calls Mail Order Magic

"Hello, is that Mail Order Magic?"

"Yes sir!

The products we sell

Make your spell

Turn out well

And we never tell.

"No ingredient is too rare for us to find.

Magic Fleeces, we've got sheep, goat,

and synthetic. For travel, flying carpets,

broooom-broom sticks, and

vacuum cleaners. Yes sir!"

"Look here, I sent you an order and

the delivery was incomplete. Where

is the frog's leg?"

"We don't handle that sort of organic

material. As I recall, it was a FRESH

frog's leg. No way, Jose! It's the

freshness factor; tadpole tails, lizard's

tails — no problem. But FRESH frog's

legs, sir, that's quite a different

*thing — they **hop**!"*

"Well, what about the shepherd's eye?"

66

"Yes sir, shepherd's pie—packed it myself."

"Not a shepherd's pie. I want a shepherd's eye!"

SLAM!

Rita telephones the Wizard

"Wizard. I am not talking to you!"

Rita telephones Shepherd Scubs

"Hello, it's Rita here. How are you doing?"

"Baaa-aa-aad, Rita love, Caaa-aa-an't seem to see any point in anything."

"You need some company. Put on the radio. I'm helping my dad in the library just now, but I can come and visit you tomorrow morning."

"OK, dear. Bye Byyyeee."

Princess Princess telephones the Kingdom Library

"Hello, I am calling to confirm my ascent of the Kingdom Library today. May I use the lift afterwards?"

King Kid telephones the Wizard

"Hello and shut up! Where is my spell?
This is an emergency! The concert is in
two days' time! . . . Oh . . . Really . . . OK
tomorrow . . . your house at teatime . . . Bye bye."
King Kid was relieved. "I had better get
organised to be a proper bossy king. Yipppeee!"

King Kid telephones the Goody Goody Two Shoes

"Hello, I am afraid that King Kid will be unable
to attend rehearsals today. He has broken
his neck. Goodbye."

King Kid telephones The Royal Tailors

"Mr Plush. Are the alterations
finished? . . . Good . . . Yes, send
it to the palace."

King Kid telephones Jay Cloth

"Hey Jay! It's K.K. . . . Today, OK to
play? . . . Eh! . . . Pay! . . . No way!"
King Kid hung up. "C.U.J.R.4.8!*"

In fact, as Spike had pointed out, he mused, after he had taken The Elixir, there would be a number of people who would be 4.8. But then again, he patted Spike fondly, there would also be a number of people who would not be 4.8.2.!

Detective Sergeant Lily Tightgrip telephones the Wizard

"Not up to anything silly, are we Wizard?"
"Me? Up to anything? Nothing!
Absolutely nothing. Promise.
Nothing! Absolutely! Bye."

All Heart Hospital Tannoy System

"Can the person who left a frog in
Casualty please pick it up."

The Wizard picks up the telephone . . .

*4.8.2. = for it too.

Chapter 17

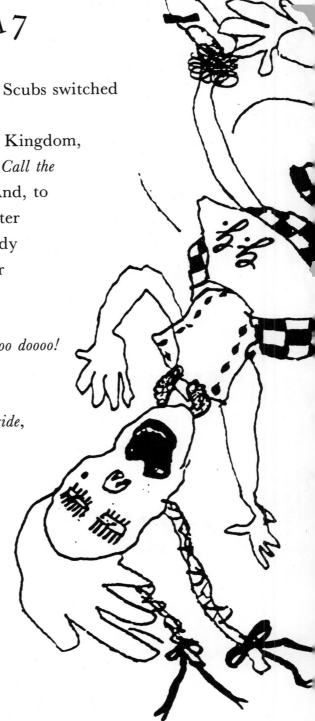

Shepherd Gra-a-assy Scubs switched on the radio.

"Tra-la-la! Radio Kingdom, dum te dum! This is *Call the Stu Tonybarry Show*. And, to begin with, what better than the Goody Goody Two Shoes with their latest record?"

Lala lili aaaaaah dee doo doooo!
What is ever on TV,
I don't care.
Whoever is playing outside,
Does not compare
With
How I love
Tidying up my room
For you, Mummy!
Right now, Mummy!
All you kids
Will have to wait
In a queue

Outside our gate
Because I am
Skipping up the stairs
Two by two.
It is my delight
To do this for you!
To sweep and scrub!
Sweep and scrub
Scrub and sweep
Scrub and sweep
To make it all neat
To make it all neat
For yoooo, Mummeeee!

"Listeners, All Heart Hospital has just been on the line to ask if the person who left a frog in their Casualty Department could please pick it up! . . . Now, who will be next on the Tonyphone? . . . Hello . . . Hello Mr Magic!"

"Hello, Stu! Starting tomorrow, I have two wonderful ingredients . . . I mean JOBS . . . jobs to fill! The first is a unique opening for an arthritic frog."

"What sort of opening? Not a dead end I hope! Ha ha!"

"Oh, no, Stu! It's an opening for a security frog!"

"Fill us in, Mr M, do."

"The only problem is that the boss, who wears a crown, has a frog shelter with a very low ceiling. Obviously, a hopping frog would be out of the question, but a legless frog would be perfect. Any frog that is keen . . . "

". . . could have his legs chopped off!"

"That's right, Stu. And I'd supply green bandages."

"Well, Mr Bad Spell, if that's for starters, what's for dessert?"

"I am looking for someone special, Stu. Someone who is capable of devotion to the Royal Family . . . blind devotion . . . or, even more precisely, half-blind devotion."

"Please conclude Mr M, before I throw up."

"OK, Stu, I need a frog with one foot in the grave and . . . a shepherd with no sheep to keep an eye on!"

Shepherd Scubs picked up the telephone receiver and dialled. And so did a well-meaning person from All Heart Hospital.

Chapter 18

A L L
H E A R T
HOSPITAL
Confidential

Dear Shepherd Scubs

Further to your conversation
with the Wizard, we will expect
you for your pre-op at 1.00 pm on
Saturday.

THE ALL HEART HOSPITAL CLOCK
STRIKES ELEVEN

As Princess Princess ascends the Kingdom Library, Rita and her dad are discussing the conversation they'd had with her, particularly her offer to teach Rita Social Climbing.

It is football morning and King Kid is in goal, writing his Press Release about tomorrow's Palace Christmas Concert.

fOr THe pREsS

1St roola to roK tHE kINgdUm

WE HaV biN LuKEE EnuF

TO CHat To tHiZ ExCLusIF PrOPEr

bOssiE KING

ANd Rok stAr. WE aRE GobSmaCKeD.

hoW iz it pOSibiL toBE Az koOl az HIm??

	LiKEs	**haTeS**
mUSiC	miNE	tHE GOoDy GOody 2 sHoeS
Color	BLak	sKooL cULuRs
cLoTHiNG	cRoWN	SkOoL YUniFOrm
FoOd	ROsTe pOtAToeS	SkoOl MAsHed pOtaToEs

StAr sine: KinG KiD

Preparing herself for the late shift, Detective Sergeant Lily Tightgrip is doing her morning sit-ups.

At Scubs Crossing, during a green light, Rita finally made it to the kitchen and slammed the door shut. She'd had to fight her way through crazy hordes of Christmas shoppers to get into the house and across the hall. "Whew! Hello Gip! Where's Shepherd Scubs? Is he still in bed? I'll go and see." She took a deep breath and opened the door. "To the staircase!" and threw herself back into the crowds.

King Kid was in a limousine with Frank Page, *Daily Curious* reporter, and Samantha Snap, photographer. They asked him for his comments. And they wanted to take his picture on location! King Kid did not know what they were talking about. But they said all would be revealed when they arrived at their destination.

King Kid had always wanted to be in *The Daily Curious*, but today, he had other worries. "Spike, do you think these two are impostors? Has my mother employed them as spies? She must have opened the package from The Royal Tailors and found my studded leather suit. . . . Oh! And the Goody Goody Two Shoes must have grassed that I didn't go to their soppy rehearsal. Oh, Spike, she knows! . . . Well, as long as I get to the Wizard's at teatime, I shall be safe."

Meanwhile, King Kid thought it best to try and befriend his captors. "Have you two met Spike the Cactus? Do you know this cactus is very naughty? He forces me to do all sorts of naughty things. . . . You may like to do a story about him."

The Wizard had just asked Shepherd Scubs and the bewildered frog to sign an agreement to become ingredients. "And, how would you both like to star in a film as well? You'll be famous."

Princess Princess was soaking in industrial detergent whilst reading the newspaper.

HOPPING MAD
BLIND WITH RAGE
GIVE HIM A FOOT
AND HE TAKES AN EYE!
Big Baddy begs blood in Beastly broadcast.
Blooming bounder blunders . . . etc.
Detective Sergeant Lily Tightgrip finished her 300 sit-ups.

scoop—All Heart Hospital. "Oh, Spike. Hospital! I hate hospitals. This is worse than I thought. My mother has lured me here. My own mother is having me King Kidnapped!"

Rita made it back down to the kitchen. "Gip, where's your pal? Something's wrong, I can feel it." Gip nudged Rita. "What's this, girl? A letter?" Gip nudged Rita again. "Why! You want me to read it don't you . . . All Heart Hospital? . . . Pre-op! Come on Gip, we're going to get to the bottom of this. Think you could try herding some shoppers?"

Detective Sergeant Lily Tightgrip started her 500 press-ups.

THE ALL HEART HOSPITAL CLOCK
STRIKES TWELVE NOON

A surgeon and a vet agreed to
co-operate to prevent the Wizard
carrying out the operations on his kitchen table.

Two trolleys speeded towards the Operating Theatre.
The Wizard was scrubbing up. He was excited. "At last
I will be able to get on with The Elixir. And on with
being crowned Cosmic Architect. I wonder if I have
time to eat lunch before the operations start."

The Daily Curious reporters, Page and
Snap, brought King Kid to the scene of their

"I'm right! Spike, they are gagging meeeemmm. They are going to drug me so that I will have to let Dame Bertha Innuendo kiss me! aaaAAAaaahh!"

Frank Page sharpened his pencil.

Samantha Snap loaded her camera.

Princess Princess switched on the TV, anxiously awaiting the news.

THE ALL HEART HOSPITAL CLOCK
STRIKES HALF PAST TWELVE.
In the Operating Theatre,
lunch was wheeled out.

Detective Sergeant Lily Tightgrip grimly
jogged to her headquarters.

A nurse put a hand on King Kid's shoulder.
"Now," she said, "off with these filthy football boots
and on with this nice clean face mask."

"This is the KBC News at one o'clock. Just hold it there doc! Hello viewers. This is Mike Furst, filming an historic occasion live from All Heart Hospital for the One O'clock News. This frog," he pointed, "and this shepherd . . . Hello there!" He shook hands. ". . . are going to give a leg and an eye for their King, respectively . . . And with us this afternoon, I am honoured and just a little frightened to have, King Kid . . ."

Whilst King Kid was waving desperately, hoping that the Wizard or someone in his class would realise that he was being held hostage, Mike Furst continued, ". . . King Kid, here to meet his donors for the first time."

King Kid whispered to Spike in his pocket, "First chance we get, we'll make a break for it."

87

COSMIC
PRIVATE DATA
THOUGHTOMETER
INSIDE the Operating Theatre.

Mike Furst
KBC News

King Kid

Samantha Snap
News
Photographer

I asked the vet
with the pretty
green eyes for
a private
interview, but
she refused and
I had hoped

Will my mum go
as far as brain-
washing me?
It's a bit much,
even for her...
   All
I had hoped

Pity the vet
found me
hiding under
the frog's
covers.
I had hoped

) HOPED . . . HAD HOPED . . .HAD HOPED . .

to ask her out
for dinner.
I wonder if
there are any
other
possibilities.
It's difficult
to tell with
these face
masks ... but
I like taking
risks.

for was not to
have to sing
with the Goody
Goody Two Shoes
and not to be
kissed by
that big
woman. It's
not fair . . .
''It's all your
fault, Spike!''

to take a
prize-winning
photograph.

Victor Victor
Film Director

Oh, hurry up!
I've hired
this operating
theatre and
the delay
is costing
me money.

The Wizard

Frank Page
Daily Curious
Reporter

I wish they
would get on

**Grassy
Scubs**

with it.

I had hoped

I had hoped

I had hoped

AD HOPED . . . HAD HOPED . . . HAD HOPED

''zzzzzz
zzzzzzz
zzzzzz''
 Frog

to have the
missing
ingredients,
make
The Elixir
and be
Royal Wizard
by supper
time.

to get a
scoop but my
editor is not
sure that
this story
is horrid
enough.

to have a
cheap day
shooting
*Amputation
Wish IV*, but
this room is
too crowded.
Who are all
these people?
That shepherd
looks a bit
of a wimp,
better get
some make-up
on him.

Rita Lovely

I had hoped

. HAD HOPED . . . HAD HOPED . . . HAD HOP

to stop this
operation.
Oh, if only
I'd got here
earlier but
I had to
fight my way
out of
Scubs Crossing
and find a
taxi. Then the
driver didn't
know the way
and we got
stuck in a
traffic jam
and when we
finally got
to the
hospital the
taxi driver
didn't have
any change
and I had to
run into a
shop and stand
in line to
get some and
then I had to
wait in the
hospital
reception
where
I had hoped
someone could
tell me where
the operation
was being
done and then
I missed the
...st and had

hundred-and-
forty-seven-
stairs-to-reach-
the-operating-
theatre-on-the-
eighty-second-
floor!
I had hoped

. . . HAD HOPED . . . H

to rescue
Shepherd Scubs
and the frog
but now,
the theatre
is so crowded
I can't get in.
How can I save
them?

Chapter 20

"Shepherd Scubs! Doctor! Nurse! Persons! Let me in! Let me in!" Rita banged on the operating theatre door. "This is awful! I can't hang about doing nothing! This is driving me up the wall! Up the smash-crash-bash-walloping wall!"

Meanwhile, in the corridor, two doctors met for the first time.

"Up the wall! That's it!"

Rita ran down the corridor. The two doctors fell in love.

Chapter 21

Fifteen minutes later, at Police Headquarters, Detective Sergeant Lily Tightgrip listened to the report on her walkie-talkie. "Two Social Climbers have over-stretched themselves, Sir . . . er . . . Madam, attempting an ascent of All Heart Hospital. They've reached the 43rd floor."

This was serious. Several plans ran through Detective Sergeant Lily Tightgrip's mind. She decided on the giant police trampoline. She would have to bring them down herself. Collecting her loud hailer and crash-helmet, she sprinted off to the scene of the crisis.

Things were even worse than she anticipated. The Social Climbers had reached the 62nd floor. She climbed on top of the police van and switched on her loud hailer.

"This is Detective Sergeant Lily Tightgrip. Stay where you are, Social Climbers."

She put her portable telescope to her eye to see their response. She was horrified. They were shaking their heads and continuing to climb.

She took up the loud hailer again. "This is a serious matter. Have you permission to climb that hospital? I warn you, climbing hospitals for no good reason is an arrestable offence!"

They shook their heads even harder and continued to climb.

Detective Sergeant Lily Tightgrip sighed deeply and surveyed the scene. The giant trampoline was in position. The streets were full of people looking up. Ice-cream vans were doing a roaring trade. Office workers, holding radios, were leaning out of windows. The situation was getting out of control—she had not organised it. She picked up her loud hailer.

"Citizens—please try to show a bit of discipline. Now. Small people at the front and tall people at the back, then everyone will have a good view. And that includes you, lorries! Small cars at the front, big vehicles at the back . . . And remember," she added, "to leave a gap to let the sandwich and soft drink vendors pass amongst you. We don't want anyone fainting, do we? I am going to bring these two down myself. Off with my boots! We don't jump on trampolines with dirty boots on, do we? Up this thirty foot ladder . . . puff, puff. Here we are! Ready. Steady. Go! Wheeeee!"

She jumped off the ladder and landed perfectly in the middle of the trampoline. She spoke calmly into the loud hailer.

"Ladies and gentlemen, excellent first bounce. Here I am parallel with the 20th floor. OoohhhHooo!" She lost her balance and spun head over tail into an accidental somersault. She held her skirt down firmly over her knees and righted herself. The crowd applauded. She couldn't help but smile. Detective Sergeant Lily Tightgrip hadn't smiled in a very long time. As she passed the 50th floor, she couldn't help herself—she hadn't felt so popular in years—she tried a triple backwards somersault and double pike. The crowd cheered. She was just about to attempt a double jack-knife-submarine-divebomber in reverse when she realised that she was passing the two climbers. Her smile vanished. "Come down immediately!" she shouted. "Jump! And that's an order."

They shook their heads.

Mike Furst
KBC News
This is very
boring. I wish
the doctors and
the Wizard would
stop arguing and
make a start.
This room is
getting stuffy.
I wonder if the
window is open.
Oh my . . .
It can't be . . .
I could have
sworn I just saw a
foot outside the
window! This
is the 82nd floor.
This could develop
into an off-
the-wall-flat-
as-a-pancake-
sorry-to-
interrupt-
this-broadcast-
NEWS-FLASH-
situation.
Oh, goody!

COSMIC
PRIVATE DATA
THOUGHTOMETER UPDATE
INSIDE the Operating Theatre

The Wizard
These people
are wet
do-goodies

Samantha Snap
Photographer
Oh, goody.

King Kid
Goody.

GOODY . . . GOODY . . . GOODY . . . GOODY . . . C

I'll gather
the team
together and
we'll sneak out.

Someone cares!
Rescued!
Spike, we are
saved!

Smashing
picture . . .

''Look here,
doctors and
nurses, if
anyone chooses
to hang outside
an eightieth
storey window,
that's their
affair. Will
you kindly get
on and make a
start! No,
they will not
have a dangerou
accident! Igno
them and they'l
go away. It's
just a couple of
window cleaner
showing off . .

Frank Page
Daily Curious
Reporter
Page 2, really!
I told him. I
told the Editor.
This is a human
AND animal
interest story!
If I don't get
scoop this
week I'll
never be . . .
Not so fast
Frank, my old
son, you may
still be in
business . . .
Goody gum drops.

Victor Victor
Film Director
''Cut, cut, cut 1.''
Time is money
honey and my
clock is ticking
dollars down the
drain. I'm not
interested in
problems. I want
action.
''Action!''
My PA wants a
word in my ear.
''Whisper,
whisper.''
What arm outside
the window?
Oh, goody.

Frog
''zzzzzzzz
zzzzzzzz''

Shepherd
Gra-a-assy Scubs
''zzzzzzzz
zzzzzzzz
zzzzzzzz''

DY . . . GOODY . . . GOODY . . . GOODY . . . G

Where's my
portable phone?
'' Sorry nurse!
Hello Editor
What about this?
Two helmetted
figures are
hanging outside
the 82nd floor
. . That's right
TERROR NURSES
IN JACK HOSPITAL
Yes, I'm sure.
Helicopter on
roof in two
minutes . . .
Come on, Sam,
but be quiet
about it. I
don't want to
lose this scoop.''

An arm outside
this window.
''Whisper,
whisper.''
*Fall to His
Death Wish IV.*
Great idea.
Come on, crew,
we're out of
this dump!

CHAPTER 22
OUTSIDE the Operating Theatre window

sssssS SSSS SSSSMMMM
aaaaAAAAAAa

"Ready, Rita?"
"Yes, Princess."
"Geronimo!"

MMMmmmmmm
aSSSSSHhh

Rita and the Princess smashed through the window and swung into the Operating Theatre.

Detective Sergeant Lily Tightgrip, close on their heels, landed on the window-sill. Taking control of the situation, she raised the loud hailer, "Doctors and nurses, sedate these two miscreants!"

The doctors and nurses picked up their instruments and approached the breathless Social Climbers.

Rita tried to speak. Waving her hands, she panted, "You don't understand . . ."

"We understand perfectly," Detective Sergeant Lily Tightgrip bellowed. "Come quietly. Forward men, but take care — Social Climbers can be dangerous."

Princess Princess took Rita's hand and whispered, "Leave it to me. I'll sort out this misunderstanding." She called out, "Detective Tightgrip! Don't you recognise me? I don't mean to pull rank or anything. It's only that we find ourselves under such duress . . . I am Princess Princess."

"You a princess!" Detective Sergeant Lily Tightgrip retorted. "Impossible — you're filthy."

King Kid, hiding under an operating table, recognised the voice. "Spike! My sister has come to rescue me, even though I used her lipstick as fake blood when we were playing cowboys."

He ran over to the cluster of hospital staff who were closing in on the two captive climbers.

"Stop! This is an awful mistake. My sister has come to rescue me from being King Kidnapped and forced to sing with the Goody Goody Two Shoes," he protested. "She is the princess. She's a dirty princess, that's all. Just because you're dirty on the outside doesn't mean you're bad on the inside. Think of a potato!" But, as usual, nobody listened to him.

He tried to talk to them individually, but they paid no attention and continued to obey Detective Sergeant Lily Tightgrip's orders. He tried pulling them, pushing them, dragging them by their clothes, and jumping up and down on their toes, but they merely shook him off. He slumped on the floor, nearly in tears. He was too short to see what was happening. He could hear an army of feet shuffling towards his brave rescuers and his brave rescuers trying to explain something about not giving an eye and a leg for some recipe. Were they all deaf?

Detective Sergeant Lily Tightgrip refused to believe anything the climbers said. She said she'd never in her life heard such a bad excuse for breaking a window and that cleanliness was next to godliness, so they were obviously very bad indeed.

"There's nothing for it, Spike. Christmas presents or no Christmas presents. If a sister tries to rescue a brother, even if she is a teenager and a girl, then a brother must try to rescue a sister.''

King Kid *Spiked* every grown-up bottom he could see. And Spike was a rare Guatamalan Sleeping Juice cactus!

The doctor raised his syringe as Rita pleaded, "We have come to save a lezzzzzzzzzzzz.''

". . . and save azzzz," Princess begged. "zzz zzz zzzzzzzzz.''

They both slumped to the floor.

And then the doctor fell over.

The vet fell over.

One by one, the nurses fell over.

King Kid pretended to fall over. He was not keen to be the only person left awake with a policing person obsessed with cleanliness — he hadn't washed behind his ears for most of December.

Detective Sergeant Lily Tightgrip was dumbfounded. There was a heap of sleeping people on the floor and an old man and a frog snoring on the operating tables. And, yes, there was one other noise. She pulled back a screen.

The Wizard was sitting on the floor, sobbing. Detective Sergeant Lily Tightgrip pulled out her notebook. "We meet again, Wizard. And what have you got to do with all this?''

The Wizard fainted.

Chapter 23

"Tra la la, Radio Kingdom . . . Dum te dum!"

"This is Stu Tonybarry with the Two O'clock News.

"We apologise for yesterday's breakdown in transmission. *The Daily Curious* helicopter crashed into our On-the-spot broadcasting unit outside the All Heart Hospital. We would like to extend our best wishes to The Daily Curious reporters, the KBC news team and the Victor Victor Films crew, all of whom will be spending Christmas in hospital.

"Today, at the High Court, Detective Sergeant Lily Tightgrip prosecuted the Wizard for Tasteless Cooking. He has been sentenced to being selfless. For the rest of his life, he will be compelled to do good deeds and never tell anyone.

"Rita Lovely and Princess Princess have been awarded the Order of Brave People for their daring hospital rescue yesterday.

"Gabriel Scubs, one of the Wizard's ingredients, has become the oldest student at Kingdom University. Mr Scubs, an ex-shepherd, says he has found a new

purpose in life due to his ordeal. He is studying to become an optician.

"The frog who almost lost a leg at All Heart Hospital and found itself at the head of The Spell Scandal has won the hearts of the people. The frog, who is recovering from shock in a puddle in the hospital car park, will be housed in the Fairy-tale Fountain in the Cottage Industries Shopping Mall. You will be able to see the frog for yourselves as you do your last minute Christmas shopping.

"And good news for all you sheep lovers. The city has been presented with a new flock. The Police Department has established a Sheep Shepherding Squad led by Detective Sergeant Lily Tightgrip. They'll

be easily recognised in their distinctive yellow woolly jumpsuits and mini-capes. Giant trampolines will be installed to enable the sheep to bounce to pastures new.

"And now ladies and gentlemen, I am passing you over to this year's Palace Christmas Concert."

"Merry Christmas everybody!" bellowed Dame Bertha Innuendo with a huge smile. "I am sorry, but I have some bad news. Unfortunately, the Goody Goody Two Shoes are having to take their afternoon nap, so they won't be able to join us. I know King Kid must be especially disappointed, as he was going to sing with them . . . Sorry K.K. . . . However, I have asked my good mate JAY CLOTH and the boys to stand in . . . Take it away . . . K.K."

Oho, oho I am a King Kid
But I am also
The slowest
at running in my class.

Heeeeees a King Kid.

But I am not
a drip kid.
I hide behind the couch
When there's kissing on TV.

Notta drip kid.

Oho, oho I may be a little stroppy
But it's really just for show
And I need a cuddle sometimes
Just don't let my mummy know.
I do-on't lie
I'm only ever kidding
But yes, it's true
I was a page at a wedding.

Oho, oho I am a King Kid
And my bike has stabilisers.
But I'm not a drip kid
Although I'm wearing shorts now

I usually wear long trousers
lo-oong trousers!
Oho, oho I am NOT a wic-kid—
I am VERY nice.
When I get a present
I don't ask the price.
Sometimes
You grown-ups
Should take
Your own advice.

OOOOOOOOOOOO OOOOOOOOOOOO

(Rhythm slows and lights darken, spotlight on K.K.)

Listennn
To your kids
We have
Our problems too-oo.
Don't want
To-have-to-talk
To-a-cactus —
Just waaaaant,
Want-to-be-hearrrrrd
By
You-oo-ooooooooooooooooooo!

109

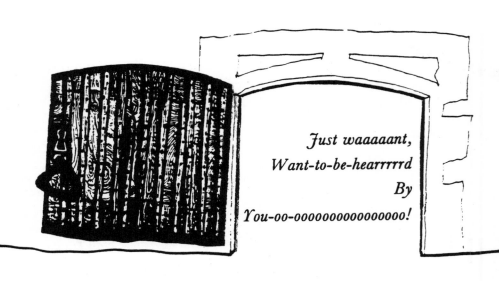

Just waaaaant,
Want-to-be-hearrrrrd
By
You-oo-ooooooooooooooooo!

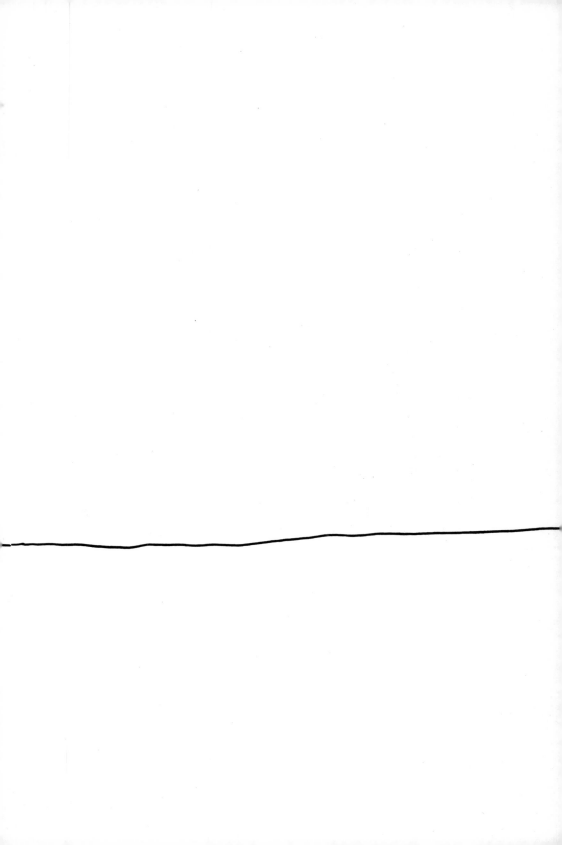